Disney
Winnie the Pooh

It's Fun to Learn

What's That Sound?

One bright morning, Tigger woke up feeling extra-bouncy.

"What a splendiferous day!" he exclaimed. Tigger knew there was only one thing that could make the day better, and that was spending it with his friends.

As he bounced off, the *boing, boing, boing* of his tail echoed through the trees. Soon Tigger heard another sound in the Hundred-Acre Wood. It went *splish, splash, splish.*

"That must be Pooh and Piglet playing a game of Pooh Sticks!" Tigger said happily. But when Tigger reached the bridge, his friends were nowhere in sight. "Pooh Boy! Hey, Piglet Ol' Pal!" Tigger called. He leaned over the side of the bridge and looked down into the water. "Nope. Nothin' there," he decided.

Suddenly—*splash!* Water shot up from the stream and drenched Tigger's face. "This needs some investigatin'!" Tigger declared. "And investigatin' is what tiggers do best!"

Tigger made his way down to the stream bank. For a moment, all was quiet. Then a school of fish leaped out of the water with a loud *splash.*

"Hey, cut that out!" complained Tigger.

He shook himself dry as a family of ducks waddled up to the stream. They fluttered their wings and kicked their feet in the water, splashing Tigger all over again!

"Hey, you splishy-splashy guys!" he called. "Have you seen Pooh and Piglet?"

"Ribbet, ribbet!" answered the frogs.

"Glug, glug!" said the fish.

"Quack, quack!" replied the duck.

"Could you say that again?" asked Tigger.

"Ribbet, ribbet!"

Tigger leaned closer, trying to understand.

"Glug, glug!"

Tigger leaned some more.

"Quack, quack!"

Tigger lost his balance.

"Drip, drip." Tigger climbed out of the water.

Tigger continued along the path. As he neared Rabbit's garden, he heard something that made him smile. "Sounds like Ol' Long Ears is whistlin' while he works!" Tigger said.

Tigger was looking forward to surprising Rabbit with a great big bounce. But when Tigger got to Rabbit's garden, there was no one there but a scarecrow.

"Say!" exclaimed Tigger. He looked at the scarecrow suspiciously. "That wasn't you whistlin'—was it?"

The whistling started up again. This time Tigger noticed it was joined by the sound of leaves rustling in the trees.

"Oh!" Tigger said to the scarecrow. "You weren't talkin'—the wind was!"

But moments later there was a noise Tigger couldn't explain. This one went *creeeaaakkk!*

It was the creaking of the wheel on Rabbit's old wheelbarrow as it started to move. The faster the wind pushed the wheelbarrow along, the louder the earsplitting *creeeaaakkk* became!

"Whoo-hoo-aaaah!" Tigger cried as the wheelbarrow scooped him up and carried him off.

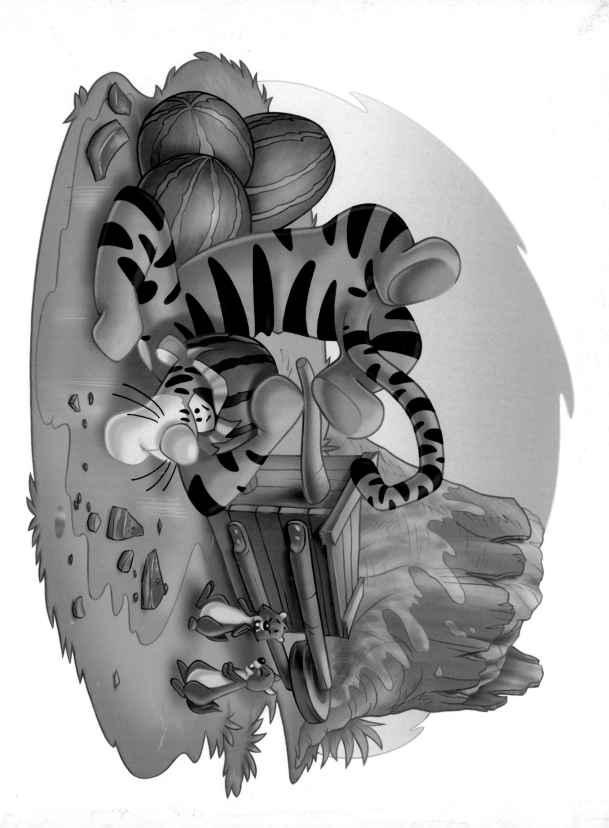

Thumpity, thumpity, thump! The wheelbarrow bumped down the hill. Then—*CRASH!*—it hit a pile of watermelons.

When Tigger climbed out of the drippy mess, he was greeted by a chorus of chitter-chattering.

"What are you laughin' at?" he asked a pair of pesky chipmunks.

"So that's where you're hiding!" declared Tigger triumphantly.

He bounded up to the cloth and tried to push it aside. But the more the blanket flapped, the more tangled Tigger became.

Tigger landed on the ground, tangled in a miserable heap. "Well, don't just stand there," he told the chipmunks. "Help me out of this!"

Next, Tigger stopped at Eeyore's stick house. He poked his head inside, but Eeyore wasn't at home. Tigger drooped with disappointment. "How am I supposed to have an adventure with someone when there's no one to have an adventure with?" he wondered.

Pitter patter, pitter patter. Raindrops began to fall on Tigger's head. Tigger decided to go inside Eeyore's house until the storm passed. *Drip, drip, drip!* Eeyore's roof began to leak.

"Hmmm," Tigger thought. "Maybe I've had enough adventure for one day."

Boom! Thunder shook the sky. "Tiggers do not like storms!" Tigger said nervously. Then he heard a *squish!* "Oh, no!" moaned Tigger. "What is that?" *Squish, squish, squish!* Whatever it was, it was getting closer!

Tigger squeezed his eyes shut. "Maybe if I pretend to be asleep, whatever it is will just go away," he told himself.

"Tigger, wake up!" called Roo. "I've been looking everywhere for you!"

"Roo!" Tigger cried, hugging his buddy. "Am I glad to see you!"

"Mama sent me to get you," Roo explained. "You're supposed to come to our house for a rainy-day picnic."

"Well, what are we waitin' for?" Tigger asked.

So the pair bounced and squished their way back to Roo's house as fast as they could.

The inside of Kanga and Roo's house was cozy and warm. Best of all, Pooh, Piglet, Owl, Eeyore, Rabbit, and Kanga were all there waiting.

Tigger was grateful to have found his friends at last. But no sooner had he settled into a chair than he heard a loud whistle.

"Did you hear that?" he asked fearfully.

"Why, Tigger dear," said Kanga. "That's just the teakettle boiling."
Still, Tigger couldn't relax. He thought Pooh's rumbly tummy was more
thunder. And he was convinced the *creak, creak, creak* of Kanga's rocking chair was
Rabbit's wheelbarrow sneaking up on him again.

After lunch, Kanga served tea and cookies. Tigger tried to enjoy his dessert, but the clinking of the cups and saucers seemed especially loud. Even his own munching was giving him a headache!

The contented friends sat back in their chairs. Owl and Rabbit sighed, happy and full. Roo, Pooh, and Piglet yawned, ready for a nap.

"Isn't it lovely to spend a nice, quiet afternoon together?" Kanga asked.

"Quiet?" Tigger replied. He looked positively worn out. "This has been the noisiest day of my life!"

Fun to Learn Activity

Cling-Clang-Bang! I was busy investigatin' sounds today! Can you bounce back through my story and find the things that made those tiggerific sounds?

Go outside and listen carefully. How many different sounds do you hear?